My Life as an Muslim American Teenager Book 1- Freshman Year

By- Dalia M. Morsy

My Life as an American Muslim Teenager – Book One: Freshman Year

Table of Contents

My Life as an American Muslim Teenager – Book One: Freshman Year

Arabic/Islamic Meanings

Chapter 1- First Day

It's tough being the new kid in school. You sit alone at lunch every day; have no partners in P.E, and everyone just keeps staring at you like you're an alien from another planet. Well, let me introduce myself. I'm Hanadi Ahmed, and I'm in 9th grade at Palm Bay High School. My family just moved from Sacramento, California, to Palm Bay, Florida, and boy let me tell you- it was tough! The moving vans driving cross country with our belongings, while we took an airplane so we could get there right before the trucks did.

Here's another thing about me- I'm Muslim. That means I believe that there is no God but Allah and Prophet Muhammad (The last Prophet) is his messenger. I also pray 5 times a day. At sunrise, which is Fajr, at early afternoon, which is Zuhr, at late afternoon, which is Asr, at sunset, which is Maghrib, and at late night, which is Isha. Plus, we believe in all the prophets, give charity as much as we can, believe in all the religious books, fast for 30 days during the Islamic month of Ramadan, and travel to the city of Makkah for the pilgrimage around the Kaabah. Since I'm in my teen years, I have to wear the Hijab, which is a scarf covering your hair and neck. It took me a while to get used to it, but soon it was comforting to wear. People always stared and stared at me whenever I was outside, but I did not care. So, my first day at Palm Bay High was yesterday.

I woke up at 5 am, prayed Fajr, and ate a nice breakfast. Then I got dressed and left for the bus stop. A few other kids were there, too. When I walked up, they all stopped what they were doing to stare at me. I tried my best to ignore it, but the whispers and snickering I heard behind me made me feel uneasy. When the bus finally arrived, I felt relived. The ride was short and before I knew it, I was there. As I got out of the bus, I just stared at the school. Palm Bay High was HUGE! I felt as my heart dropped to my feet. "Keep calm, Hanadi. Just keep calm." I told myself.

I walked into the school and tried to find the main office, so I could pick up my class schedule. Luckily, it was close by, so I found it in no time. As I walked in, the secretary gave me a strange look, but then plastered a fake grin on her face. "Hello, and welcome to Palm Bay High School! What can I do for you today?" She said cheerfully. I just smiled and told her what I rehearsed in the mirror about 100 times. "Hi, I'm Hanadi Ahmed, and I'm in 9th grade. I just came here for my class schedule so I can get through my first day here." The woman then looked through a couple of drawers and then pulled out a thin folder. "Here is a pamphlet that has a map of the school, a list of the school counselors, special clubs and events, and of course, your class schedule. I hope you have a great school year!" I thanked the secretary and walked into the courtyard of the school.

I was just amazed at how big the school was. Students were walking from class to class, and staring at me as they walked by. But I did not care a bit. I looked at my class shudele for the first class I was going to attend. "Okay, my first class is Algebra 1 with Ms. Jones." I said nervously. After looking at my school map, I found out that Ms. Jones class was on the 2nd floor, and that it was about to start in 10 minutes! I put my papers back in my folder, sighed, and found the closest staircase and raced up those steps as fast as I could. Ms. Jones class was at the end of the hall, and when I finally got there, I was 2 minutes away from being tardy! I thanked Allah for making me get to class on time, made a Duaa (prayer), asking to make the rest of the day easy, and walked into my first class.

Chapter 2 – New Class

I made it to class just in time! Ms. Jones was about to start the lesson, but personally, I wouldn't mind if I missed some of it. Math is generally not my strong suit. I'm much better in Language Arts and Science. Those subjects are just so interesting to me! Ms. Jones looked up and smiled when she noticed me. "Hello! You must be Hanadi

Ahmed! Welcome to Algebra 1. Please, take one of the empty seats in the back." I walked to the back of the room, aware of the 20 pairs of eyes on me. As I settled in, Ms. Jones started the lesson. While she was explaining how to solve an algebraic expression, my thoughts drifted to my old town that I used to live in, Sacramento. I thought of all my friends, my old school, and my best friend, Ridha.

Ridha and I have been best friends since 5th grade, and we did almost everything together. We went to the same school, sat together at lunch, and we were even in the same classes! We always passed notes to each other about other kids, the class, and our teachers! But we got caught one time, and the teacher read the note in front of everybody. It was so embarrassing! Then a loud, sharp voice snapped me out of my daydream. "Hanadi, I asked you to solve the problems I gave out to everyone. Are you ok?

You were smiling and staring off into space." Ms, Jones said. I felt myself blush as I noticed everyone staring at me again. "Sorry, Ms. Jones. I'm okay. It's just hard trying to adjust to a new school." I explained politely. Ms. Jones smiled. "Well, okay then. Back to work, everyone!" She announced. I started working on my math sheet. It was kind of hard, but I finished right on time. Once Ms. Jones class let out, I looked at my schedule for where to go next. "Language Arts with Mr. Brown." I took a deep breath and walked off. Thankfully, Mr. Brown was a very nice teacher and praised me over and over about my Reading and Language Arts skills. I was proud of myself for the essay I wrote in class. It was about persuading school officials that kids need more P.E time. Mr. Brown gave me an A+! When I walked out of his class, I felt like I was on Cloud 9!

The next class on my list flooded all the happiness out of me. "P.E! OMG, I really don't feel like running laps or doing push-ups right now!" I said out of frustration. I had no other choice, so I treaded off to P.E. My coach was Coach Thomas. He was a big guy, with huge muscles and totally fit, but he did not take no for an answer. When one of my classmates didn't want to do the warm up excirces- which I think are a complete waste of time, Coach Thomas yelled at her and made her run 20 laps around the Football field. And that field is HUGE! "Boy, I hope I don't do anything to tick this guy off." I thought to myself. Then he made us do 20 push-ups, 10 laps around the field, weight lifting, and stretching techniques. Then P.E was finally over. The kids who were slacking were forced to take showers, and thank god I wasn't one of them!

I was nearly jumping for joy when the next thing on my schedule was lunch break.

As I walked into the humongous cafeteria, I gasped. The cafeteria was even bigger than my old school's! Since I didn't bring lunch, I got on line to get a food tray. What they were serving looked kind of decent, but I was bringing my own lunch from home starting tomorrow. After I picked up my food, I scanned the room for an empty table and found one all the way towards the end of the cafeteria. I sat down and began to eat. A few minutes into my meal, I heard someone clear her throat behind me. "Excuse me, do you mind if I sit with you?" I looked up and saw it was a girl around my age smiling at me. "Of course you can. Are you new here?" I asked. The girl sat across from me and then shook her head. "No, I'm not new.

I used to have friends to sit with, because I used to be a part of the most popular clique in the school, gorgeous and popular. But they kicked me out, and I've found myself alone almost all the time." The girl looked a little bothered, so I tried to comfort her. "Well, you don't have to be part of a clique to be my friend, and I like you, no matter what. What is your name, by the way?" "Grace. What's yours?" I smiled. "I'm Hanadi." Grace gave me a big smile. "Hanadi? That's such a pretty name!" I laughed as I cleared my lunch tray and we left the cafeteria together. I know that this is the start of a great friendship, I could just feel it!

Chapter 3 –

Bully Trouble

I checked my schedule for my next

class while Grace checked hers. "Hey!" She
exclaimed. "We both have U.S History
together! Isn't that epic?" I double checked
my list and saw that she was right. "Well, we
better hurry if we want to catch Ms. Smith's
class!" I exclaimed. When we entered, Ms.
Smith greeted us warmly. We both chose a
seat near each other as the class began. Ms.
Smith began to talk about World Wars 1 and
2 and the Civil War. I grew bored very fast,
and I could see that Grace was, too. Even a

kid in the back of the class was dozing off! I grabbed a piece of notebook paper and scribbled a note and carefully passed it to Grace. She read it, smiling and writing a note of her own on the bottom. Before she could give it to me, a tall, pretty girl who was sitting behind me began to cough.

Her coughing then magically stopped when Ms. Smith turned around and looked at the class. I also turned around and shot the girl a dirty look. She looked familiar, and then it dawned on me. She is part of the Gorgeous and Popular Clique! She was trying to get Grace in trouble! Ms. Smith walked over to Grace's desk, and she did NOT look happy. "Grace, are you passing notes in my class?" She asked. Grace looked at me, then at Ms. Smith. "Um, yes Ms. Smith. I'm sorry." Ms. Smith then looked at the note and I cringed as her eyes got huge. Then she was looking at me. "Hanadi, are you also passing notes?" I put my head down and said "Yes, I was passing notes as well." Ms. Smith looked very angry. She walked to the front of the room.

I held my breath, hoping that she would not read the notes in front of the whole class! But she did something even worse. "Grace, Hanadi, please see me after class." She announced. I suddenly got very nervous. I was praying that we would not get detention! As class finished, the kids began to leave for the last class of the day- Science. The girl who got us in trouble, Ashley, gave us a smug grin as she left the class with a mile wide smile on her face. When the room was empty, Ms. Smith told us to bring chairs to her desk so we could talk to her. As we sat down, Grace and I exchanged nervous glances as we put our attention to the teacher. "Girls, why would you write such things about me and this class? History is stupid, and when will Ms. Smith stop blabbing? Do you think those were good things you wrote?" Ms. Smith looked at both of us, obviously disappointed. "I'm very sorry! That will never happen again, and we will make sure of it! We both understand that History is important and that we need to respect our teachers." I said, hoping that we wouldn't get in any more trouble. Ms. Smith glanced at Grace, who had her head down. "Grace, do you agree with what Hanadi has told me?" Grace looked up, sighed, and said yes. "Good then. I hope we have an understanding here. And if this ever happens again, it will be detention for the both of you!!" Ms. Smith yelled.

As we left her classroom to go to our last class of the day, Earth Science with Mr. Martin, we thought about what happened with Ms. Smith. "That girl, Ashley, wanted us to get in trouble. She just faked a cough so Ms. Smith would get distracted and notice us! I hate her so much!" I said, letting all my anger finally spill out. "It's not you," Grace said sadly. "It's me that she hates. She wanted me to get in trouble." I looked at Grace, puzzled. "But why would she hate you, you are the kindest person I've ever met." Grace just looked at me. "Remember I used to be a part of the Gorgeous and Popular Clique? Well, Ashley, our leader, thought I was prettier and more popular than her. So they kicked me out, and nobody even stood up for me!

My popularity went down the drain as soon as I got kicked out. Now I'm as popular as a week old moldy sandwich." Grace sighed, and tears were coming out of her eyes. "Everybody hates me! And now that I got you in trouble you probably hate me too!" Grace had the full waterworks on. I tried my best to calm her down, and gave her some tissues.

"No, Grace, I don't hate you at all! You are my only friend at this school. What happened today was a lesson for both of us. No more passing notes in class!" I said cheerfully. Then we left to Mr. Martin's class.

When we finally got there, there was a happy feeling that suddenly came to me. Mr. Martin looked like a very kind teacher, and the classroom had a soothing atmosphere. When Mr. Martin noticed us come in, he said, "Girls, you are 10 minutes late! What happened?" I gulped and nervously told him, "I'm sorry, Mr. Martin. We got into a bit of trouble in our last class. That's why we are late. We promise it won't happen again." Mr. Martin smiled. "Ok girls. Find a seat, and get to work. Grace and I found seats next to each other and settled down.

The teacher started the lesson, it was Earth Space Science. Earth Space Science is really easy for me. I enjoy learning about it, and I get very good grades, too. We were now learning about Earth and its layers: The crust, mantle, inner core, and outer core. Then Mr. Martin played a video about it for about the topic for the rest of the class. What a great way to end my first day of school. After class let out, it was finally time to go home! Grace then ran up to me. "Hey, you never gave me your number. Let's exchange numbers so we can text each other!" she said. I thought it was a great idea, so I gave her my number, and she gave me hers. "Thanks Hanadi. My mom is here to pick me up, so I got to go. Is your mom here too?" Grace asked. I shook my head. "No Grace, she's not here. Both of my parents work. I have to take the bus home. See you tomorrow!" I said.

As I was walking to the bus stop, I saw a really cute boy come to the bus stop as well. He had blue eyes and wavy brown hair, and when he glanced at me, I felt myself blush! When he passed by me to get on the bus, he winked and smiled at me. I just froze in my steps and my insides felt all weird. Was I developing a crush on this boy? And if I was, is it Haram to have these feelings? I felt so confused as I boarded the bus and rode home.

Chapter 4 –

Boy Drama

As the bus pulled up on my street, I hopped out and pulled out my house key. I unlocked the door and went inside. I kicked off my shoes, pulled off my socks and hijab, and went upstairs to change my clothes. Once I had changed into a more comfortable outfit, I went downstairs and fixed myself a snack. Then I watched some TV. But my mind kept going to my new crush. I was kind of nervous, wondering what my parents would say and if I should even tell them at all. So I text Grace for help. She told me that I should tell them if it was bothering me so much. But then she asked who it was. I told her it was this boy with wavy brown hair and blue eyes. A few minutes later, she text back, saying that he was Adam Sanchez, and he was in her Algebra 1 class. A lot of girls already had a crush on him.

Once I heard that, I felt my heart drop to the floor. Great, just great. I thanked Grace for her help and started to do my homework. Soon, my mom came home from work. "Hello Hanadi. How was your first day of school? Anything exciting go on?" She asked. I just looked at her. There was no way I was going to tell her about Grace and I almost getting detention by passing notes and Ashley ratting on us. And I didn't want to tell her about my new crush, either. So I just said, "Oh, hi Mom. Everything is fine. School was great, and I made my first friend here. Her name is Grace." Mom gave me "The Look", which is a certain stare she gives someone when she thinks they are not telling the truth.

I took a deep breath and told her everything that happened today: Meeting our teachers, Meeting Grace, getting in trouble, the note passing and of course, the boy drama. Mom was quiet for a few minutes, then she said, "Hanadi, you must remember to treat your teachers with respect. You cannot pass notes in class and you cannot daydream. That is just showing the teacher that you don't care about what they are teaching you. Do you understand?" I sighed and said, "Yes, Mom. I understand. I promise it won't happen again." Mom smiled. "Great, Hanadi! I'm happy to hear it. Now, let's talk about this boy drama.

It's ok to have a crush. It's just human nature. But no dating or anything like that, ok?" I nodded my head. Just thinking about that made me blush. "Hanadi, just remember this," Mom said. "When a girl is alone with a boy, the Shaitan (Devil) is also there with them. This is a Hadith from the Prophet Muhammad. Ok?" I nodded. Mom hugged me then left the room to start dinner. I finished my homework, and then it was time to eat. When I came downstairs, I saw that my dad was already home! Mom cleared her throat and said, "Hanadi, I already told your father what happened and he agrees with me. No more getting into trouble with your teachers, ok?" I nodded and then looked at my Dad. He said, "Hanadi, what your mom told you about your crush is true. Just be careful, ok?" I said yes, and sat down at the table to eat. After our meal, we all prayed Isha together and then watched some TV. After that, it was time to go to bed.

As I laid down to go to sleep, I made a Duaa (Prayer), hoping that tomorrow will be a better day. The next day, I woke up a little late and rushed through my breakfast, changed out of my pajamas so I wouldn't miss the bus. I ran as fast as I could to the front door, said bye to my parents, and ran to the bus stop. And guess who was already there? Adam! Out of all people, my crush has to be the only person alone with me at the bus station. My heart was pounding.

He turned and looked at me. "Hi," He said. "Oh, hi Adam." I said. "How are you doing?" He looked down at his feet. "I'm good." This conversation was so awkward! I was actually glad when the bus arrived. As I sat in my seat, I hoped that today would be a better day than yesterday. When the bus arrived at school, I met up with Grace and hung around the courtyard of the school until the bell rang. Once it did, we all went to our classes. The day sped by quick, and soon it was lunch time. When we were walking to the cafeteria, a piercing noise shot through the air.

I looked around, and saw that it was the fire alarms. The principal was running out of his office and telling everyone to go line up outside. The faint smell of smoke filled the air, and that's when I knew we were in trouble. The teacher that was trying to calm down the principal called 911 and told all the gathered up students to come outside immediately.

Chapter 5 – The Fire!

As we were being led out of the school building, Grace was worried and looked liked she was about to cry. "Grace! What's wrong? Hopefully nobody got hurt." I told her. Grace looked at me with red eyes. "That fire alarm freaked me out! What if we weren't able to get out of the school! We could've died!" I looked at her, and said

"Grace, the good thing is that we are out, safe, and alive, ok? And that nobody got hurt." Grace looked at me and smiled. "Hey, you're right. As long as no one is hurt or dead, everything will be okay! Thank you for making me feel much better." I smiled back. "Anytime for a friend Grace. Anytime." Soon the Fire Department arrived and checked out the fire. We found out that it was a small fire in the cafeteria kitchen. No was hurt, but the whole cafeteria smelled like smoke. So we had lunch outside in the courtyard today. When I finished my meal, I saw Adam walking towards us. My heart began to pound, but I tried my best to stay calm. "Hey Grace, hey Hanadi," He said. "Are you guys ok? You still look pretty shaken up." I looked at Grace. She still looked pretty scared. "The fire alarms scared us to death. And to think that there was an actual fire in the school? That's kind of scary if you think about it. But thank god no-one was hurt." I said. Adam smiled. "That's great. Catch you guys later." He called as he walked away.

After lunch was over, the principal made an announcement saying that school will be closed for the rest of the day. Awesome! I love early releases! I said bye to Grace and walked to my bus stop. Luckily, the bus was already there, and I got in and took a seat. As the bus drove home, I looked out the window and thought about today's events. Once I was finally home, I let myself in and got a snack to eat. About an hour and a half later, Mom arrived. She saw the look on my face and came to talk to me. "Hanadi, is everything ok?" she asked. I just sighed.

"Why can't one day of school go by where there isn't any drama?" I yelled out in frustration. My mom just looked at me for a few seconds, then said, "Woah! What happened now?" I just cleared my throat. "I've been home for about four hours now because there was a fire at our school. We had early release. I mean, I don't mind getting out of school early, but just thinking that we could have been killed in that fire makes me feel scared! Alhamdulilah (Thank God) no one was hurt!" I said. Mom's face was frozen. Then she said, "Wow, my god, I can't believe that happened! Are you sure you're okay?" I smiled at her, and said "I think I'll live. Thanks for making me realize that everything will be alright." Mom smiled back. "That's great to hear. Now what about helping me with dinner?" She asked. "That would be awesome, because with two people working on dinner, it will be done faster, because I am starving!" I exclaimed. Then we started cooking. About 30 minutes later, the dinner was done, and it was looking good! Rice with mixed vegetables and beef seasoned with garlic. When Dad finally came home, we set the table and started to eat. The food was delicious.

As we were eating, I told dad about what happened at school, and he had the same reaction as mom did! He asked the same questions, and looked kind of frightened. I just looked my dad in the eyes and said this: "Dad, Alhamdulillah no one was hurt. Just the cafeteria smelled like smoke and also got damaged, so we had to eat lunch outside. But Allah (God) was watching over us, and we are all ok." Dad relaxed and smiled. "Hanadi, I'm just glad you're okay." He said. Soon it was time for bed, and boy, I was exhausted from today's crazy event. At least tomorrow is Saturday, and I can sleep in. That's why I love weekends!

Chapter 6 –

Friend Trouble

On Saturday, I woke up at 12 noon. I mean, I was physically and mentally exhausted from yesterday's drama, so can you blame me? After I got out of bed, I brushed my teeth, my hair, changed into house clothes, and went downstairs. Mom was already awake, and Dad left for work. Mom was home because she had Saturday and Sunday off. When I walked into the living room, Mom looked up from her computer and smiled. "Good Morning! Or should I say

Good Afternoon?" She said with a chuckle. "Hey, good morning Mom." I said. I went into the kitchen to make myself lunch. I was starving!

A few minutes later, I was sitting on the couch, eating a tuna sandwich with sour cream and onion chips- my favorite! After I swallowed that down I watched some TV. Then my phone started to ring. I looked at who it was, and it was Grace. I picked up, and said "Hey Grace, whats up? Hows your weekend going so far?" Grace was quiet for a moment, then said, "Well, im not doing anything exciting, but I called because I want to know if you want to go to the mall with me. Can you?" I thought for a second, then asked my mom. "Mom, Grace wants to go to the mall with me. Can I go?" Mom smiled. "Of course, but be back before midnight!"

She said. I got back on the phone with Grace, told her I could go, and left for the mall. I hoped I had enough money to buy some cute clothes! As I was driving, (I got my drivers permit not too long ago) Grace text me. I waited until I was in the mall parking lot to respond. The text said, "Hey Hanadi! You at the mall yet? I just got here about 5 minutes ago!" "Wow, she got there fast!" I thought as I got out of the car and walked towards the entrance of the mall. Once I was in, I saw a familiar face waving at me a few feet away. It was Grace! Once I reached her we hugged, then started to walk around. "Where were you? You had me waiting like forever!" Grace exclaimed. I looked at her and said, "I don't live as close as you do to the mall, remember?" Grace frowned. "Oh,yeah. I forgot." But then she perked up again. "So, let's get shopping! I hope you are ready for a big shopping spree!" I smiled. "Well, let's get moving! I'm all ready to shop to my heart's desire!"

Soon, Grace and I were moving store to store, buying clothes, accessories, and shoes. It was the most fun I've had since we moved here. We went to Rue 21, Forever 21, Macy's, Aldo, and a few other stores. But before we left something happened that made me very angry. We were walking towards the exit of the mall when I saw someone that looked familiar. It was Ashley and two other Gorgeous and Popular girls. They were also headed towards the exit but when they saw us, they stopped and just stared.

"Well, well, well. If it isn't the Lame Squad. Hey crybaby, how are you and your dumb friend? That's who you chose to replace me? Wow, you really are just pathetic." Ashley said. Her two minions were agreeing to everything Ashley said, and laughing along, too. That's when I just blew up. I was tired of watching Grace get bullied by these girls, and I was tired of being insulted just because I was her friend. I gave those girls a cold, hard stare and then started to let out my anger. "Ashley, why are you such a bully? What did Grace do to you guys that you think you can treat her like that?" Ashley tapped her finger on her chin, pretending that she was thinking, and then said: "Well, she betrayed our clique. If you didn't know, Hanadi, when you're in a clique, especially one like ours, you are not supposed to hang out with non-clique people." I looked at her like she was crazy. "Why? Is it against the law to have a lot of friends?" I asked, waiting for her response.

Ashley was just standing there with her mouth open, not saying a word. I gave her the same smug grin that she gave me when we got in trouble for note passing. "Oh, I see. I thought so." Then Grace and I walked towards the exit, got in the car, and drove home. We were feeling pretty good about ourselves. After I dropped Grace off at her house so she wouldn't have to walk home, I drove home. When I walked in, my family was already eating dinner. "Hey! I thought you guys would at least wait for me!" I said, serving myself and sitting down at the table. Mom looked at me. "So, how was the mall with Grace? Did you guys have fun?" She asked. "Well, we did have fun shopping," I said, pointing to the pile of bags I brought home. "But these girls that bully us at school, Ashley and her 2 drones, who are part of the clique Grace used to be in, were bullying her! They were so mean, insulting her and calling names. I just could not stand there and watch her get bullied, so I stepped in and stood up for her. I told them off, and we left them speechless." Mom and Dad were quiet. Then Mom said, "Wow Hanadi. I'm proud of you. Standing up for your friend like that, that was a wonderful thing to do!" Dad agreed. I smiled, thanked them, and got ready for bed. It was 1am! When I took a shower, got in my pajamas, and went to bed, I thought about today as I drifted off to sleep.

Chapter 7 – The Dance

On Sunday, after I woke up, which surprisingly was at 11am, I ate breakfast. I planned to stay home so no drama would be in my day, unlike yesterday. So, after breakfast, I started to clean my room a little bit. Yesterday I almost tripped on a pile of shoes that I had on the floor! About an hour later, my room was as clean as a freshly bathed baby. And it smelled like it too, because I sprayed lots of Lysol and air fresheners. After that was out of the way, I watched some TV. New episodes of my favorite shows were on, and I wasn't missing them! Later on in the day, I called Grace to see what she was up to on this boring, gloomy day. Literally, I had nothing to do, and it looked like it was going to pour outside.

It was time for lunch! A juicy burger with tomatoes, lettuce, onions and pickles had me feeling bloated in about 5 minutes after eating it. About 2 hours later, I helped my mom get dinner ready. As we cooked, we talked. Mom looked at me and said, "So, Hanadi how was your first week at your new school? Did you meet any new friends besides Grace, and Adam?" I just sighed. "No, just Grace and Adam. I wish more kids would be willing to be my friends." Mom brought the dinner plates to the table, and I helped her. "Hanadi, Habibti (Sweetheart) it will take longer than a week to make new friends. If you are patient, Allah will bring new friends your way." Mom said. As we were eating, Dad nodded, his way of saying he agreed to what she was saying.

The next day in homeroom, the teacher was passing out flyers for a dance called "Freshman Frenzy." It was going to be in April. "Oh, no!" I moaned. Grace looked at me. "What's wrong, Hanadi?" She asked. "This dance called the Freshman Frenzy; I won't be able to go!" I wailed. Grace suddenly got worried. "Why won't you?" I just started at her. I thought I already explained this to her! "Remember, I'm Muslim? I can't dance to music." Suddenly a snobbish voice interrupted our conversation. "Oh well! That's too bad for Hanadi! Boo hoo." Ashley mocked. My cheeks burned with anger. Grace put a hand on my shoulder. "Hanadi, just don't worry about it. The dance is in April, and we're in January. That gives you 3 whole months to think about it." I smiled at Grace. She always looked on the bright side of things. But deep down inside, I felt really sad that I probably would not be able to go to the dance with my friends. I mean, is it haram if I go but don't dance, just to hang out with friends?

That is something I would have to ask my parents. Later on, when I was walking home from my bus stop, I was practicing what I was going to say to my parents. "Mom, Dad, my school is having a dance called the Freshman Frenzy. Can I go?" I thought for a moment, but then I knew my parents would never say yes if I ask them that way. So I thought of a different response: "Mom, Dad, there's a dance at my school coming up called the Freshman Frenzy. I know we are not supposed to listen to music or dance but if I just go to hang out with my friends, is that okay with you guys?" Now that's a question I know I will get a better answer with. When I finally got home, I fixed up a snack, watched a movie, read a book, and just waited for my parents to come home.

When I heard their car outside, I suddenly got very nervous and sat down on the couch near the front door. "Salam, Hanadi! How are you?" My parents greeted me as they came in. "I'm good, how are you guys?" I asked as I tried to hide a nervous smile. My mother gave me "The Look." That means she knows I am hiding something. "Well, Hanadi, how was your day? Better than yesterday?" she asked. I looked at her and saw right away what she was trying to do. She was trying to get whatever I was hiding out of me. "Okay, fine. I was hiding something from you. In April, there's going to be an event called the Freshman Frenzy. Well, not really an event, more like a dance. I know that we are not supposed to listen to music or even dance, but can I go with my friends just to hang out? I promise I won't dance or anything like that. Please!" I held my breath as I looked at my parents faces. They were surprised, trying to take in whatever I just told them. Then they walked off to their bedroom. I heard whispering. I made a Duaa (Prayer) in my head, hoping that they would let me go.

When they returned, the looks on their faces said it all. Mom cleared her throat and began to speak. "Hanadi, you know that if you go to this dance, you are committing many sins! Dancing? Music? And boys will be there, too! I'm sorry, the answer is no. you can't go to the dance." I looked at my Dad with a pleading look on my face. But he just agreed with everything my mom said! I was so angry; I ran to my room and slammed the door. I began to cry as hard as I could, hoping I would get a different response from my parents. But I didn't. I cried myself to sleep.

Chapter 8 –
Meeting Andrea

When I woke up the next morning, I was in a pretty decent mood. But while I was eating breakfast, I noticed both of my parents staring at me. Then I remembered what happened last night. The memories flushed my entire good mood down the drain. I just finished eating and went to my bus stop. When I got to school, as soon as I saw Grace, I told her the bad news about the dance. Grace looked devastated, because she wanted to go with me and hang out. But just then, a great idea came in my mind. "Hey Grace, since you don't want to go to the dance alone, lets both stay. We can have a sleepover at my house. Isn't that better than some stupid dance? Grace looked away and said, "But what if all the other kids find out that we won't go to the dance? They will think we can't get a date or something like that." I calmed her down, and said, "No one is going to say anything like that, Grace. Just don't worry. You will see that everything will be ok." Grace smiled. "Thanks for making me feel better, Hanadi. You really are a great friend." She gushed. It felt good to make a fellow friend feel better.

The rest of the day passed by quick, and right before dismissal, the teacher was telling us about our upcoming standardized tests in a few weeks. I suddenly became very nervous. I'm absolutely horrible at those tests. But the real reason that I'm worrying is if you fail the test, you can't pass the class. If you fail a test in, let's say Algebra. You don't get a credit for the Algebra class and you have to redo the test! It definitely wasn't like that in Middle school! Why does High school have to be so hard! Then an unfamiliar voice broke me out of my daydream. "Hi, I'm Andrea. Could I sit with you tomorrow at your lunch table? I'm new here." I said yes right away, because I remembered how I felt without any friends, and being the new girl in school. So the next day, Andrea joined Grace and I at lunch. "Grace, this is Andrea. She's new at this school." I said. "Hi, Andrea! I'm Grace. Hanadi and I would love to be friends with you!" Andrea smiled. She had a nice smile, and I think she is going to be a great friend. Lunch flew by quickly, and we got ready for class. We were laughing all the way to homeroom.

Andrea was such a good friend, and she was really funny, too! Andrea had a different homeroom teacher, so we said goodbye and walked into our class. When school ended, I went home and completed my homework. Tomorrow was Saturday, so I had plenty of time to study for my SAT tests and plan for my sleepover. But I had to ask my parents first. I hope they were still not angry about the whole dance thing! The next morning, I ate breakfast early and studied for my tests. After hours of studying, eating lunch, texting Grace, and studying some more, it was dinner time. I was nervous about asking my parents for the sleepover. When we all sat down to eat, I looked at my parents nervously. I didn't know where to begin. Mom was picking at her food, and eating the low carb foods only. I found that strange, because she never did that before! I looked at her stomach. It was a bit bigger than usual. A thought crossed my mind, but I quickly got rid of it. She probably just gained some weight. I looked at Dad. He had already eaten his whole plate, and he was on his phone. I cleared my throat, stood up, and prepared to tell them about my plan. "Mom, Dad, I've been studying non-stop today because I have an SAT test in February. I think that I will do very well if I keep up the same study schedule."

Dad looked at me with his famous glance. "Hanadi, are you trying to get a point across, or are you trying to ask us something?" I smiled. How did he know?

"Well," I said, fidgeting around with my fingers, "After SAT'S are over there is going to be the dance in April. Since I can't go-and I completely understand why, can I hold a little sleepover with my friends that night? Since I'm not going, they don't want to go either. We all thought that a sleepover is more fun and entertaining." My dad looked at my Mom. She nodded to show her approval, and then tried to get up from the table. My dad rushed to her side, which I found strange, and helped her walk to her room. As they were walking, I noticed that my mom's stomach looked very big.

When Dad came back, he sat down next to me. "Hanadi, we should have told you earlier, but we did not want to interrupt your studies. Your Mother is pregnant." I almost fell out of my chair. "WHAT? Pregnant? When is it due?" I asked excitedly. "Late April or Early May, around there. But that is just an estimate." My Dad said. "And, by the way, you can have your sleepover." He added. My eyes widened with excitement. "Wow! Thanks Dad! I can't believe that all this time, I never noticed that Mom was pregnant. I guess I was too busy with school." I said. Dad smiled. "I guess so. But just imagine, Hanadi! You will be a big sister! It's what you've always wanted!" He said. I just smiled. "Yeah, I guess. So Dad, I'm really tired. It's been a big day. Good night." I said.

Dad just looked at me. "Good night, Hanadi." He said. The next day came fast.

Sunday we usually don't do anything productive, so we just sat around and watched TV. Dad does not go to work on Sunday, so he was home with us. Deep down inside, I felt kind of excited that we would have a new family member. I thanked Allah (God) and hoped that the baby would be healthy and happy.

Chapter 9 – The Reading SAT'S

February soon came. Everyone in school

was freaking out. Then I remembered why. SAT'S were just in a few days! I could not believe how fast time flies. But like they always say, Time flies when you're having fun. I felt well prepared for the tests, so I wasn't freaking out like everyone else. Grace and Andrea ran up to me. "Hey, Hanadi did you see that the dates for the SAT'S are already posted?" Grace practically screamed. "I'm so nervous and-hey, why are you not panicking like everyone else, including myself?" She asked. I just looked at her. Panicking does not solve your problems, it just creates bigger ones. "I have been studying day and night, because my parents will not let me have the sleepover if I fail, okay?" I said.

Grace actually looked scared. "Oh, okay. No need for the dramatic scary stuff. I'm sure we will all do fine. Right, Andrea?" Grace asked. Andrea smiled, but it looked sort of forced. "Hey, yeah, don't worry guys. Everything's going to be ok." She said. Then she just walked away to her homeroom. Grace and I just looked at each other. Something was up with Andrea. And we were going to find out what it was.

On the way to class, Grace and I stopped by the SAT board to see our dates. We both had the same days-February 4th and 5th for the reading, and February 6th and 7th for the math. I was hoping that those days would pass by quickly, but they did not. On the first day of testing, February 4th, we would be doing the first segment of reading. We went to the computer lab down the hall from our classroom. Grace was not in my same lab, but Andrea was! She looked like she was crying. Then the teacher who was directing the test walked in. "Ok, kids. Today is the first segment of the SAT Reading test. You may not have any electronic or recording devices with you. If you are found with these, your test will not be scored. Also, if you share any information about this test on social media websites like Twitter, Instagram, Snapchat, and Facebook, your test will not be scored. Any questions?" she asked, looking at all of us. Nobody said a peep. "Ok then. You may begin."

I opened my computer program and began the test. I was surprised, because the test was surprisingly easy, and I finished second. Andrea was first. We could not leave the room until everyone was done, so we just waited. Once everybody was finished, we left the computer lab and met up with Grace at lunch. We both talked about how easy the first part of the reading test was. Andrea was quiet, and looked kind of sad, like she was about to cry. "What's wrong, Andrea? You looked like you were crying before the test began. Are you ok?" I asked. Andrea finally blew up. "It's my parents! They threatened to take my phone and laptop if I fail this test." Then she burst into tears. I just looked at her, and tried to comfort her. "Oh, Andrea! Do not underestimate yourself! Do not worry about what your parents told you! My parents say things like that to me all the time, and I always try my best and pass because I don't want to lose my things!" I told her reassuringly. Andrea smiled at me. "Really? Well, I did try my best, so I think I will pass." She said, cheering up. Grace and I looked at each other. We both felt proud for cheering up a fellow friend in need. After lunch, we went to our last classes of the day, and went home to prepare for part 2 of the reading test.

When I was at home, I sat in my room studying until my parents called me down for dinner. When I was downstairs, Dad motioned for me to come in the kitchen. "Hanadi, your mother has been very tired lately, and I was hoping that you could help me serve the dinner. Can you? Or are you studying for tomorrow's test?" He asked. "Well, I was studying, but I'm done for tonight. I would be glad to help you and Mom." I said with a big smile on my face. Dad smiled back. "Thank you, Hanadi. You know this means so much to us, with your Mom pregnant and everything." He said. I looked at Mom. She was sitting at the table, with her hand on her belly. She also looked very tired. When she noticed that I was looking at her, she smiled and said, "Thank you, Hanadi. Thank you for all your help." I just blushed and said, "Oh, it's no big deal. Now let's sit down and eat!" The next day at school was part 2 of the SAT Reading. I didn't really sweat it, because the 1st part was easy. We all went to the same computer labs. The same kids were there, and so was Andrea. But she looked calm and cool, probably because of what we told her yesterday. The time flew by, and before we knew it, the Reading SAT was over!

Kids everywhere were smiling, laughing, and cheering. I was one of them, and so were Grace and Andrea. But then I froze in my footsteps. "Guys, we are not done with our tests yet! Math is tomorrow, and the day after that!" I yelled, draining all the happiness out of me. I am horrible in math. That was an understatement!

I was terrible, absolutely terrible. Grace also stopped cheering and frowned. She wasn't a pro in math either, so she wasn't looking forward to the math SAT. But Andrea practically jumped 2 feet in the air and cheered. "OMG, math is tomorrow? I'm awesome in math! It's my favorite subject! Woohoo!!!" She yelled. A few kids walking down the hall stared at her like she was a crazy person, and then walked away. "Oh, Andrea, you are good in math? I never knew that." I said, feeling a bit jealous. "Yeah, I am. I was honor roll in math through elementary and middle school. I guess math comes easier to me than reading does." Andrea explained. "Oh, wow. Good for you." Grace said with a hint of jealousy in her voice. Andrea flipped around to glare at Grace and said, "Well, I guess somebody is a tiny bit jealous, aren't they? But you just can't help it, can you?

That's just the way you are." Grace walked up to Andrea, took her hand tightly, and said, "Well, I'm not the one who was crying like a little baby because you think you were going to fail the reading SAT."

Andrea's eyes grew large. "How do you know that? You were not in the same computer lab as me!" She shrieked. Grace gave her a sly grin and said, "I have my sources. Almost the whole school is talking about it. Gossip spreads like wildfire, you know." That's when I had it. I've had enough of this. "Guys, stop fighting, and let's go to lunch. NOW." I said. Andrea and Grace had a startled look on their faces, but listened to me and walked to the cafeteria together. As we

were walking, a thought crossed my mind.
What if they didn't get along during my
sleepover, or worse-what if they didn't get
along at all? But I quickly got rid of that
thought and entered the cafeteria. When we
sat down on our usual table, Grace and
Andrea sat away from each other. I just rolled
my eyes, and looked at both of them. "Guys,
why are you both acting like this? Remember,
we are best friends! We are supposed to be
happy for each other, no matter what. No
jealousy, no anger, no nothing. So, can you
guys please be nice to each other?" I asked.
Grace and Andrea looked at each other. Grace
sighed and looked Andrea in the eyes.
"Andrea, I am so sorry for being rude and
cruel to you. I guess I was just jealous that

you were so good in math. Can you please forgive me?" Grace asked.

Andrea's face changed as soon as she heard the apology. "Oh, Grace, I think this was all my fault. I was bragging about how good I am in math, and I didn't think about your feelings first. I am so sorry." Andrea said. She looked at Grace with a pleading look on her face. Grace smiled and said, "I forgive you!" Andrea smiled, hugged Grace, and forgave her as well. I just looked on and smiled. I felt secretly happy that they were back to being best friends. That way, when we have our sleepover, we can enjoy it and have lots of fun.

Just then, the bell rang, signaling the end of lunch and interrupting my thoughts. It was time to get back to class. When I was rushing to get to my math class, because we were having SAT prep, I bumped into Adam. He smiled, blushed, and said, "Oh, hi Hanadi. Looks like I'm not the only one in a rush to get to SAT prep. How do you think you're going to do on the math test?" I smiled. "Well, I know I won't pass with a super high grade, so I probably will get a 3 or something." I said, my palms sweating like crazy. Man, why do I get so nervous when I talk to him? Well, he is the boy that I'm crushing on, so yeah, that explains it. Then Adam said, "Well, we better get to class. And by the way, I heard that you aren't going to the dance. Why not?" I looked at him and said, "My parents said I could not go because it's haram (Bad) to go to a party and listen to music." Adam nodded and said, "Oh, ok. I thought it was because you could not find anyone to go with you." He stared at me and started to blush. Of course, I started to blush, too. As we smiled at each other, I heard our class start from the room behind us. "OMG, we've got to go!" I said. Adam and I said goodbye and rushed to our class.

Chapter 10 – The Math SAT'S

When I walked into my SAT math prep

class, the teacher glared at me.

"You're late, Hanadi. Take your seat so I can continue the class." I just looked at her and sat at my desk. There was a math formula sheet on my desk with a test worksheet. "The worksheets I have placed on your desks are practice for your SAT test tomorrow. Since your test is timed, I am going to time you. I will give you 45 minutes to complete the worksheet. The formula sheet is there to help you. Are you guys ready to begin?" The teacher asked. "Yes, we are ready." The class said. "Ok, you may start the work now." The teacher replied. We had 45 minutes, so that was a good amount of time to finish my worksheet.

And boy, those questions were hard! All these equations and decimals and algebraic functions! I felt like my head was going to explode. But thankfully, I finished 5 minutes before the time was up. The teacher then collected our worksheets, and formula sheets. Then we were allowed to leave the classroom because school was over for the day. When I got home I ate a nice big snack, and then got straight to work. Math SAT'S were tomorrow, so I needed even more studying than the reading SAT'S! After about 4 hours of studying, I completed my homework, ate dinner, and went to bed. Tomorrow is a big day!

When I woke up in the morning, I ate a nice nutritious meal. I needed brain power if I was going to pass that math test! After I was ready to go, I just studied a little more and left for school. When I arrived, everyone, and I mean every single kid was freaking out about the math test. I guess all of their parents threatened to take their electronics if they didn't pass, too! I tried to stay calm, but all the yelling and screaming from the other kids got me a little nervous. When I arrived at the computer lab, it was a different teacher than last time, and Grace was in the same room! I smiled at her as I walked to my computer and she smiled back and winked. That was our secret code for-good luck! Andrea was also in the same room, and she looked more confident than last time.

After about 10 minutes passed, the teacher handed out the formula sheets. Then she made an unexpected announcement. "Ok kids, due to a problem in the SAT computer program, we will have to complete both segments of the test today. You will have a 5 minute break between the sessions, and the results of both the reading and math will be mailed to your house in the middle of March." Then after that kids started to freak out. We didn't study for both segments! Andrea looked like she was about to cry. The teacher tried to calm everyone down, and told us we would get 20 extra points added to our test score because of the whole computer mistake. I liked the sound of that!

Everyone finally calmed down. I felt calm, too. At least we did not have to take a test tomorrow! The teacher started to tell everyone the testing rules, gave us good luck, and started the test. It was kind of easy; most of the things on the SAT were the things that I have been studying. But even if I do get a low grade, I would still pass with a decent grade because of that 20 point boost. Segment 1 was finally over, and we had a 5 minute break. I had to go use the restroom and get some water, so I did. When I came back, the break was over, and segment 2 was starting. To be honest, I found segment 2 a little be harder than the first one. But I tried my best, because my parents were counting on me. About an hour later, the teacher told everyone to stop and submit their tests. I was done alhamdulilah (Thank God) and so were Grace and Andrea. After the testing, we went to our homeroom because our teacher had an announcement to make. "OK class, you finally finished your SAT'S. Are you happy?" He asked, looking around the room. "Yes! Yes! Woo-hoo!" The class cheered. "Well, you will get your results in the middle or the beginning of March. I hope you all did great! They will be mailed to your house, so make sure you keep an eye out for the envelope and bring them to school." He said. "It's time for lunch, so go enjoy your break!

You've earned it!" We all scrambled out of the room and went to the cafeteria. Grace, Andrea, and I were all going to talk about the SAT tests. When we all got to our table, we got our food out and began to talk. "So, Andrea, was the test easy or hard for you?" Grace asked. Andrea smiled and said, "Why, yes, it was very easy for me. I'm more of a math kind of gal." "Cool," I said. "Because the test was really hard for me. But I hope that the 20 point boost will give me a good grade." Grace just looked down at her feet. I put a hand on her shoulder and said, "Grace, are you ok? Look, if the test was hard, you can just tell us, ok? We are your friend, and we care about you. Right, Andrea?"

Andrea gave Grace a fake smile and said, "Oh, yeah we care for you. Don't worry about a thing." I could tell that there was still tension between the 2 of them, but since I did not want to cause any more trouble, I kept my mouth shut. Lunch ended and we attended our last classes of the day. I was happy that the SAT'S were over because the teachers were less tense and calmer with us. They didn't pressure us anymore. Then it was finally time to go home. When I got home, I told my parents that the SAT'S were finally over. "Great, when do the scores come in?" my Dad asked. "Oh, the teachers said early or Late

March." I said. "Well, the earlier the better!" said my Mom. After dinner, I got ready to go to bed. Tomorrow was Saturday and I was glad. When I woke up the next day, it was around 12 or 1pm in the afternoon. Boy, was I tired last night! Since I had nothing to do, I just hung around the house. I watched my favorite shows, Once Upon a Time, Sleepy Hollow, and Smallville on TV for about 3 hours until my mom came and shut of the TV. Then, I text Grace and Andrea, who were just as bored as I was. It was so weird that we could not find one thing to do this Saturday afternoon. I hoped Sunday would be more productive.

Chapter 11 – The Scores Come In

When I woke up Sunday morning, I felt determined to do something productive. After I ate breakfast, took a quick shower, and changed out of pajamas, I took a nice morning walk around my neighborhood. Some of my neighbors were fixing their lawns, cleaning their cars, or talking a walk as well. I said hi to a few people I knew, and walked back home. When I got back, my mom and dad were awake and drinking their coffee. When they saw me come in the living room all sweaty from my walk, their eyes grew big. "Hello Hanadi. I can see that you went for a jog this morning. How was it?" My mom asked. I sort of smiled and said, "It was great. The real reason I went out to jog was because I wanted to do something productive today. Yesterday, I was just sitting around, watching TV, and doing nothing. I felt like I was just wasting away." Mom smiled. "That's great, honey. And remember, today is March 2nd. Your SAT scores should be coming in any day now! So be prepared!" She said happily. As she left the room, I frowned. I didn't see anything to be happy about. I was nervous, because what if I failed? But I tried to think on the bright side, and hoped that I passed. My sleepover depended on it! To get my mind off of my tests, I went to the freezer to get a nice, big bowl of ice cream. Then I went to my room and binge watched a couple of old movies until bedtime. The next day at school, I text Grace and Andrea to meet me in front of the school before class starts.

I wanted to ask if they got their SAT scores in. I was waiting for about 10 minutes when Andrea and Grace finally showed up. I just stared at them and gave them a look. "Guys, you were 10 minutes late! I wanted to talk about the SAT'S. Did you get your scores?" Grace thought for a minute, then said: "No, not yet. Remember, they said early or late March. So it could come anytime in the month! Don't spend your time worrying about it. You've got better things to do!" I smiled.

Grace always knew the right things to say. Andrea then said: "Sorry, Hanadi. I didn't get anything either. But I will tell you if I do." I said: "Thanks Andrea."

Then the bell rang. We had to get to class. But the day sped by, and before I knew it, I was home again. The minute the bus stopped in front of my house I jumped out and ran to the mailbox. When I opened it, I saw a big white envelope with my name on it! I started to freak out. Before I knew it, I was hyperventilating and I felt like I was going to faint. My mom saw me through the window and ran out to see if I was ok. When she got to me, she was out of breath and holding her stomach. I dropped the mail and ran to her side. "Mom, are you ok? You should not be running, even speed-walking! You're 8 months pregnant!" When my mom finally caught her breath, she said: "Oh, Hanadi, you gave me such a scare! When I was fixing up the house because of the baby's arrival, I heard your bus pull up. So I just glanced out the window, and saw you having a total meltdown at the mailbox holding a white envelope. Was it your SAT scores?" I just glanced at the envelope on the grass- I dropped it as soon as I knew what it was, and said: "Um, yeah. That is my scores." My mom's face perked up, and she bent down to pick up the envelope. "Come on; let's go see what they are!" Mom said as she walked back in the house. Unwillingly, I followed her. When we were inside, mom took the envelope to her desk and started to open it! I ran into the laundry room, closed the door and just stood there, heart pounding in my chest. A few minutes passed by. I heard my mom talking on the phone.

Oh no! What if I got a low grade on my tests, and she's telling my dad! I was so nervous. About 10 minutes later, mom found out where I was and opened the door. "Hanadi, why are you hiding in here? Don't you want to see your test results?" She asked. I looked at her. She didn't look angry or upset. Instead, she looked happy, and her face was glowing. Since she looked so happy, I decided to go look at scores. I wasn't expecting 5's on both tests, but I must've gotten a 5 on one of them. So I sat on the couch and opened the envelope. As I read my results, I couldn't believe my eyes! I got a 5 on my reading test and a 3 on my math. I was so happy that I started to jump up and down and scream. My mom just looked at me, and started to smile. "Wow, looks like someone is VERY happy.

You look very relieved, too." She said. I just started to laugh. "Mom, I'm not just relieved. I'm extremely relieved! I feel like a huge weight has been lifted from my chest." I said. Mom just smiled. But then I remembered my sleepover. Before mom left to get dinner ready, I asked her about my sleepover. "Hey mom, one more thing. Since I passed my SAT tests, can I have my sleepover next weekend? Remember how I couldn't go to the dance, and you guys said I can have a sleepover with Grace and Andrea if I passed my SAT'S? Well, I did! So can I have it?" Mom thought for a few minutes, then text my dad about it. I was so nervous, waiting for his reply. But when I heard her phone ding, I froze. Dad said yes! I was so happy I hugged my mom tightly until she grunted. I immediately let go and carefully looked at her. "Mom, are you ok?" I asked. She looked like she was in pain. "I'm so sorry!" Mom just smiled and patted my hand. "I'm ok, Hanadi. Don't worry; it's just that these past couple of weeks have been tough. I've been feeling very sick and my stomach has been hurting me.

The doctor said those are signs that the baby might be an early bird." She said. I just looked at her. "Early bird? What is that supposed to mean?" I asked. "Early bird means that the baby might be born early. Earlier than expected." Mom explained. I just froze right in my steps. Early? Earlier than expected? What if I can't have my sleepover? I just pushed my worries aside, because I knew I was being selfish. "Wow, mom. That's great. That means the baby will be with us very soon." I said. Mom smiled. "I know!

I get more excited just thinking about it! We have to start choosing names! 3 for a girl and 3 for a boy. Well, Hanadi, I'm going to get dinner rolling. I'll call you when it's done."

Then she went to the kitchen. After she was
gone, the look on her face when she told me
the news made me feel bad about putting my
sleepover first. When mom said dinner was
ready, I went into the dining room and ate
calmly. After I got ready for bed, I text
Andrea and Grace the news. They were super
excited, and wanted more information
tomorrow. I just lay in my bed, hoped
everything would be ok, and went to sleep.

Chapter 12 – Twins?

When I got to school the next day, Andrea and Grace ran up to me and hugged me as hard as they could. "Oh, Hanadi! Congrats! I'm so happy for you!" Grace said. "I'm so excited. Do you want a boy or a girl?" Andrea asked. I thought for a second. I hadn't thought about that yet. "Well, I would prefer a girl, but if a boy comes, I'm okay with that." I said. Then Andrea's eyes grew big. "OMG! What if it's twins?" she practically screamed. Then a flashback came to my mind. Mom's stomach did look pretty big. I think she might be having twins! "Well, Andrea we just have to wait and hope for the best." I said.

Then the bell rang, signaling the beginning of class. During all of my classes, I just could not get my mind off my mom. If she had twins, it would be stressful for all of us, mostly her. But it was also kind of exciting, thinking that one day; we would have two little kids running around the house. But a sharp, loud voice took me out of my daydreaming. "Hanadi, what are you doing?" I looked up and saw my science teacher standing in front of my desk. "Are you ok?"

I sighed, and told her what was bothering me. "My mom is 8 months pregnant and it might be twins. I just can't get it out of my mind! I know I should be excited and happy, but it's all I ever think about." My teacher's face changed. "Oh my goodness!" She gasped. "Congratulations! That's fantastic! Send your mother my regards." She said. When the class was finally over, I went to my locker to get a few things. But suddenly, I heard giggling and the click of high heels. It was Ashley and the Gorgeous and Popular girls! I tried to hide behind the door of my locker, but it was too late. They already saw me. "Oh, well hey there, loser. How are you and your loser friends doing? Ashley cackled. I just looked at her. How can these girls be so cruel? I guess that's how they are. So, I decided to kill them with kindness. "Oh, well hey there, Ashley. I haven't seen you in a while. Hope you've been doing ok. And yes, Grace and Andrea are doing fine, thanks for asking!"

I gave all of them a nice big smile, waved goodbye, and walked to lunch. From behind me I heard gasps, then lots of laughter. I turned around and saw the whole hallway laughing, and no, I'm not kidding. Every single kid was laughing so hard they were turning blue. I glanced at Ashley, and saw her face turning red, with her mouth hanging open. Her friends looked ash white and looked so embarrassed. They were probably wishing that they weren't Ashley's friend. I just chuckled and walked into the cafeteria. After I sat down at our table, I told Grace and Andrea everything. "OMG, Hanadi, you were awesome! Ashley was being her cruel, usual self and you put her in her place! No one in

school history has ever dared to do that!"
Grace shrieked.

"Well, Grace, this school has been open for only 10 years, so I personally wouldn't call that history. And that's called killing her with kindness. I had to do something, because she just walked up and started to insult you guys, myself included. So I dealt with her, and I did not have to say 1 cruel word! How's that for you?" I said. Andrea's mouth dropped open. "Wow, Hanadi. You really are a great friend. If I were in your shoes, I would not have a clue on what to do. I would have probably run away, crying! But you are so brave. Grace and I are lucky to have you as a friend." She said. Grace nodded, agreeing with her. I just smiled, and said: "Oh guys, it was nothing, really. I just wanted to defend my 2 best friends." Then the bell rang. It was time to go back to class. And I was feeling pretty good about myself. My next classes passed by fast. People all around the school, mostly the teachers, congratulated me on my new brother/sister.

I was getting pretty excited because I could not wait for my new family members to arrive. When the bus dropped me off, I ran inside and checked on my mother, who was sitting on the couch reading a parenting magazine. When she saw me, she smiled. "Hey, Hanadi. How was your day at school?" She asked. "Good. It was good. How are you?

Are you feeling ok?" I asked. S he tried to stand, but struggled. I helped her sit back down. "Mom! Do not try to stand up! You need to relax." I said. Then my eyes drifted towards her belly. It was huge! It looked like she was going to give birth any day now! I could not believe that in just a few days, I would be holding my little brother or sister in my arms. It made me feel all warm and cozy inside just thinking about it. When it was dinner time, I told my mom: "Hey Mom, its ok. Rest. You are about to give birth any day now. Let me cook dinner tonight."

My mom smiled and hugged me. "Oh, thank you Hanadi! That is so kind and thoughtful of you." She said. About a half hour later, dinner was ready. My dad was already home and kept a close eye on mom. He also sat next to her in case she needed anything. When I served the dinner, my parents eyes grew big. I guess they never knew that their daughter could cook teriyaki noodles with teriyaki seasoned chicken! But it tasted wonderful, and my parents loved it. When I finally got ready for bed, I thought about my mom. Tomorrow was already Wednesday. What if mom had the baby tomorrow, or Thursday? I was excited, but also nervous. I soon fell into a deep sleep. When I woke up the next morning, I got dressed, ate breakfast, and hopped on the bus to school. When I arrived, I received a text from my mom. It said: "Going to the doctor today to have an ultrasound. Stay strong!" I was suddenly excited. The ultrasound will be able to tell us if there are twins, and what their gender is! I text her back, saying: "Great mom! I will check on you later!" I felt happy, nervous, and excited as I went to my class. I could not wait for the results!

Chapter 13 – Phone Trouble

When I was in my 3rd class of the day, I

heard my phone buzz. Then it buzzed again. And then again. When the last text came through, I was pretty sure it was my mom. Boy, I wanted to read those texts so bad! When I made sure that the teacher wasn't looking, I took my phone out of my bag. Then I quickly read the texts my mom sent me. She was having twins, and one was a girl, and the other was a boy! I gasped, and did a little dance in my chair. I was so happy! But my teacher noticed.

She walked toward my desk, and gave me a look that meant: "I know you are texting" and held out her hand. "But, but my mom is at the doctor! She had an appointment, so she just text me how she's doing! I'm sorry if I did something against the rules of the class." I said. But my teacher was not buying it. "Hanadi, you know that there are rules against texting and usage of phones during class. Please see me after class is over." She said. Then she held out her hand again. I had no other choice. I put my phone in her hand and watched in horror as she walked to her desk and put it in a desk drawer. I felt so embarrassed that I just wanted to run out of class crying. As the class went on, I just worried about my mom, and what my teacher wanted to say to me. About an hour later, the class was over. All the other kids were putting away their books and getting ready for lunch, but not me. I had to see what my teacher wanted.

When the class was empty, I got out of my seat and walked to my teacher's desk. She was preparing for her next class. When she noticed me, she sat up straight and cleared her throat. "Hanadi, I know that you are worried about your mom, but you know that use of phones during school hours are against the rules. And you must know that your actions have consequences. You are going to have lunch inside the classroom for the rest of the week, including today." She said. I gasped when I heard what my teacher told me. No lunch in the cafeteria for a week? No eating lunch with my friends? That sounded horrible! I would have to eat alone. Then, a loud voice cut through my thoughts. "Am I clear, Hanadi?" My teacher asked. "This will make sure you will not use your phone in school. Okay?"

I just swallowed and said, "Okay." Since lunch was next period, I prepared for lunch. I was pretty bummed out that I could not eat lunch with my friends, but hey? This is Allah (God) telling me to obey the rules of school and not get in trouble again. When I sat down on my desk, I began to eat. My teacher walked over and smiled at me. "Hey, eating lunch with me isn't so bad. Cheer up, Hanadi!" She said. "So, how is your mother? Is she feeling ok? Almost all the teachers know that she is pregnant." "Well, she was having an ultrasound done today, and found out that she is having twins! 1 girl and 1 boy, and I'm so excited!" I told her. My teacher's eyes lit up. "Oh my god, that's amazing! Oh, I just had a great idea. Later on today, I will tell the teachers that your mom is giving birth any day now, and tomorrow, we will all give you gifts to give to your mother for the babies! How does that sound?" I thought for a second, and then said: "That sounds AWESOME! My mom will love it!" My teacher gave me a big smile. "Wonderful, then it's settled. I will tell the teachers later on today. Trust me; she's going to love it! Now hurry up, my next class is about to start. See, eating lunch with me is not so bad! If you would have done something horrible, then it wouldn't have been enjoyable. But it was!" My teacher exclaimed. A few minutes later, her next class filed into the room and sat on their desks. "Well, I gotta run to my next class!" I said to my teacher. "Thanks for what we did today, I really enjoyed it!" As I ran out of the class to get to my next one, I thought about my mom and all those gifts that she would receive. I knew she would really enjoy it!

Chapter 14 – The Twins Are Coming

When I got home, I ran in the house and went upstairs to my room. Hopefully, my mom didn't see me. I walked over to my desk, did whatever homework I had, and then got down to business. I wanted to calculate the number of presents my mom would be getting. I had 7 periods in 1 school day, so that meant 6 teachers. If each teacher gave 1 gift that would be 6 gifts for my new baby brother and sister. But, if the teachers gave more than 1 gift, that would be more than 10 gifts! I was getting more excited just thinking about it. But then, I heard someone coming upstairs. It was my mom! I closed all my books that I was writing in and shut off my computer. Then she finally came into my room, and she did not look happy. She had her phone in her hand, and it looked like she just got off the phone with someone. My palms suddenly got sweaty, and my throat felt tight. Then my mom began to speak. "Hanadi, I got a call from the school principal saying that you got a 1 week detention for texting in class. How could you do something so foolish? You know you are not supposed to use phones in class!" she yelled. I just stared at her. She text me in class about her doctor appointment. That was what got me in trouble in the first place! "Mom, I'm not trying to be disrespectful or anything, but I got in trouble for texting you. When I was in class, I got your text saying that you are having twins.

When I heard my phone ding, I was just taking it out to put it on silent. But then I saw your texts, and I got a little too excited. My teacher noticed and then gave me detention for texting in class. I wasn't texting anyone else, I swear!" I said. Then I noticed my mom's expression change.

"Oh, no I forgot that you were in school! I was just so excited! I sent a text to the whole family, so they can hear the great news. I'm sorry for getting you in trouble, and for getting so angry with you. Do you forgive me?" She asked. I gave her a big smile. "Of course I forgive you, mom!" Then I gave her a big hug. But she grunted in pain. I suddenly let go and looked at her face. "OMG, Mom are you okay?" I asked, super worried about her. But she just smiled. "I'm ok, Hanadi. And by the way, you can have your sleepover this Saturday. Ok?" She said. I suddenly perked up. I never felt so happy in my life! "Really? This Saturday? Thank you, mom! I love you!" Then I ran to my room and text Andrea and Grace about it. They were really excited, like me!

As I got ready for bed, I thought about the events happening in my life. The detention, my new siblings, and finally my sleepover. As I fell asleep, I dreamed of a perfect ending to the school year: My sleepover, graduation, my new siblings, and a great start to summer vacation. When I woke up the next day, it was Wednesday. Just 3 more days until my sleepover. I rushed to get ready and got to school early. When I arrived, I saw Andrea and Grace waiting for me in the courtyard. When they saw me, they ran up, overjoyed. "So, the sleepover is Saturday? We can't wait! Woohoo!" Grace shouted. Andrea smiled. "I can't wait, either. This sleepover is going to be fun! We can stay up watching movies, eating junk food, drinking soda, and do makeovers!" she exclaimed. "Hey, yeah! Makeovers are a great idea! I have mascara, eyeliner, eye shadow, blush, and nail polish. This will be awesome!" I said. Just then, the school bell rang. Time for class. We rushed to class as fast as we could. We did not want to be late! About 6 hours later, school was out for the day. I was happy, because tomorrow would be Thursday. Only 2 more days until my sleepover!

I could hardly wait! When I was home, I noticed my mom was having trouble moving around and getting the dinner ready. So, I immediately ran to her side and helped with the food. My mom was surprised, but pleased as well. After we ate, she told me to come to a corner and said: "Wow, Hanadi, I'm so, so happy for all your help. The babies might be coming any day now. So I will need your help more than ever. Thank you so much." I just smiled. Helping your mother is important in Islam. I hoped I was getting good deeds by helping her out. When I went to get ready for bed, I was very pleased with myself. I hope my family was as well. The next two days flew by so fast; that it only felt like one had passed. It was finally Saturday! My sleepover was tonight! As I put out my sleeping bag and little snacks, my mom walked into the room I was in. I was putting out some DVD's to watch later when I noticed her.

My mom did not look too good. She was holding onto her stomach and was having a hard time sitting down. I rushed to her side. "Mom, OMG, are you ok?" I asked, starting to get worried. She just looked at me. "Hanadi, I'm in labor. The babies are coming tonight! Call your father!" She said. I ran and got my phone, and called him. "Hello,

Hanadi?" He said. "Dad, Mom is having the babies! She's in labor, and we need to get her to the hospital NOW!" I practically yelled on the phone. Then my dad said: "Oh my god, Hanadi, I'm still a half hour away at work!

Call 911; get an ambulance to take her to the hospital! Text me when you get there." After my dad hung up, I called 911. "911 what's your emergency?" the operator said. "My mom is going into labor right now, with my twin brother and sister. I don't have a car, so I need an ambulance! Please, I need it as soon as you can!" I said. "Well, we'll send you one. Just stay calm, keep your mother as comfortable as possible, and please give me your address." The operator replied. I gave her our address, hung up, and ran to my mom. She looked like she was in a lot of pain. 3 minutes later, I heard the ambulance outside. "Ok, mom, the ambulance is going to take us to the hospital.

Just stay calm." I told her. Then there was loud knocking. I opened the door and 3 paramedics with a stretcher ran in and prepped her for the hospital. When they put her on the stretcher, strapped her to it, and loaded her in the ambulance, I jumped in and sat in the chair next to her. I held her hand and told her that everything will be alright. When we arrived at the hospital about 5 minutes later, they rushed in the hospital and to the ER section. I just had to sit in the waiting room while they took my mom to see the doctors. I made a duaa (prayer), called my dad, and hoped for the best.

Chapter 15 – A Perfect Ending

After I called my dad 2 more times and text him, he finally made it. I ran to him and we both hugged. Then we both sat down and waited for any news on mom. My phone kept buzzing in my pocket. When I took it out to see what it was, it was Andrea and Grace. They kept calling and texting. I just turned off my phone and tried to relax. Besides, the hospital didn't have service. About 5 minutes later, a doctor and a nurse came out of the emergency room doors and walked up to us. "Hello, are you the husband of Mrs.Ahmed?" The doctor asked. My dad practically jumped out of his chair. "Yes, that's me." He said. The doctor looked at his chart, and then said: "Congratulations. Your wife just gave birth to a beautiful set of twins. One is a girl, and one is a boy." He announced.

My dad and I looked at each other, and both said at the same time: "Can we see them?" The doctor and nurse both started laughing. "Of course you can! But not for long, because they need their rest." The nurse said. Then they lead us through the ER doors, into the elevator, then down the hall into the maternity unit. Then the doctor took us to mom's room. We had a 30 minute visit before we had to leave. When I walked in, I could not believe my eyes! There was my mom, in her hospital gown, laying in bed holding my new brother and sister! "Oh, Mom!" I said. I ran to her side and hugged her. Well, I tried to. My mom smiled. "Hanadi, this is your baby brother, Hassan, and your baby sister, Nour." She told me happily. I smiled. Those were beautiful names she chose. In Arabic, Hassan means beautiful or handsome. Nour means light. "Mom, can I carry Nour?" I asked. "Of course you can." My mom replied. So I took Nour from her hands and put her in my arms. I looked at her little face. It was so peaceful, and so pretty. I looked over at Dad, who was carrying Hassan. Mom had tears in her eyes and was smiling.

Then a nurse came into the room. "I'm sorry, visiting hours are over. You may go home and come again in the morning." She said. So we said goodnight to mom and the babies and went home. When we were there, my dad took a shower and went to sleep. But before I got ready, I text Andrea and Grace about what happened today, and that we will have the sleepover another night. Then I got ready for bed, and fell fast asleep.

The next day was Sunday. I woke up pretty early for the weekend, 10 am! I went to my dad, woke him up, and we drove straight to the hospital. Now that mom has her own room, we had unlimited visiting time. We had fun with the twins, mom was happy, and we all had a great time. Mom was able to come home on Monday. I was so excited! The next day at school, Andrea and Grace were in our usual spot, waiting for me. When I finally got to them, they practically jumped on top of me, saying: "OMG, we heard about your mom! Congrats! What are the twins names?" I smiled. "One is a girl; her name is Nour, which means light. The other is a boy; his name is Hassan, which means beautiful or handsome." I told them.

Andrea began to giggle when she heard that, then she was full on laughing. Grace joined in and soon enough, I was laughing along with them. After that, Grace asked: "When can we do your sleepover again? I really want to see your new siblings!" She exclaimed. "Me too," said Andrea. I thought for a second, and then said: "I will ask my parents, and then I will tell you guys what they say, ok?" Andrea and Grace agreed with me, and we all rushed to our classes for the rest of the school day. When I finally got home, I saw mom on the couch, feeding the twins. I was never so happy to see my mom in my whole life! I ran to her and gave her a big hug. "Oh, mom it's so good to have you back! How do you feel?" I said. Mom just laughed.

"Boy, you sure are talkative today! Is there something you want to ask me?" she asked. Wow, it's like she read my mind! But I was saying a little duaa (prayer) in my head, hoping that she would let me have my sleepover this Saturday. "Actually, yes there is something I want to ask you. Remember my sleepover? I was going to have it last Saturday, but you had the twins-not your fault. Can I please have it this Saturday coming up? Please?" I asked.

Mom thought about it for a second, then said: "Well, Hanadi, you know how busy I have been with the twins. So I will make you a deal. Take a little time out of your day to help me with the twins, and then I will let you have your sleepover Saturday. But that does not mean you only help this week and that's it!" Mom said. I hugged her, and said: "Of course I will help you, every single day, all the time! Thank you so much mom!" then I ran up to my room and text Andrea and Grace. Then I did my homework. By the time I was done, they both replied, and they were just as excited as I was. As I went to bed, I thought about the fun time we would have that night. It was going to be a blast.

Starting today, my schedule for the rest of the week was like this: School, homework, help mom. School, homework, help mom. It was ok, because I wanted to help mom out and spend lots of time with the twins.

Fortunately, the week flew by. When I woke up Saturday morning, I was almost too excited to function. I got my DVD'S out, the movies that we would be watching, and a few board games. I also cleared a space in my room for Grace and Andrea to lay out their sleeping bags. When it was getting close to 7pm- they would be arriving at 8pm, I got out the snacks and drinks. It was going to be one fun night! When I heard the doorbell ring, I ran to get it. I let Andrea and Grace inside and led them upstairs so they could set up. While they were setting up, I helped my mom with the dinner. Once it was finished, I called them down to eat.

While we were all eating, we talked about what we were going to do later on, and other stuff. "So, Hanadi, what do you have planned for us tonight?" Grace asked. "Oh, I have some movies we can watch, board games, and other stuff. But don't worry, I know you will enjoy it!" I said. "WooHoo!" Andrea cried. "Let's get this party started!" As we ran upstairs, mom smiled and said: "Have fun, girls." When we were upstairs, we changed into our pajamas, and watched a couple of movies. Then we pigged out on the snacks I brought up. By the time it was 12:30 am, we were playing board games half asleep. "Ok, guys wake up! I have one more thing I want to do.

Makeovers!" I exclaimed. A few minutes later, we were putting on eye-shadow, mascara, eyeliner, lip-liner, blush, and lip gloss. We also curled our hair. "Perfect, we look absolutely amazing!" I exclaimed. Then we settled down, and took a couple of pictures for memories. Then we all lay down to go to sleep. As I was falling asleep, I thought about all the fun we've had throughout the school year. Even though this year was over, we still had another 3 years together. And we would make the best out of them. After all….friendship conquers all!

The End

Arabic/Islamic Words in this Book

Allah- God

Asalamu Alaikum- Peace be upon you

Inshallah- God willing

Alhamdulilah- Thank God

Hassan-   Handsome,
beautiful

Nour- light

Hanadi- lovely smell

Hadith- a saying of the
prophet

Salah- prayer

Duaa- prayer

My Life as an American Muslim Teenager – Book One: Freshman Year

Made in the USA
Monee, IL
09 June 2023

35521571R00080